*To Bernard,*
*whose idea it was in the first place.*

Copyright © 1991 by Nord-Süd Verlag AG, Gossau Zürich, Switzerland
First published in Switzerland under the title *Ein ganz verrückter Nikolaustag!*

First published in the United States, Great Britain, Canada,
Australia and New Zealand in 1991 by North-South Books,
an imprint of Nord-Süd Verlag AG, Gossau Zürich, Switzerland.

Library of Congress Cataloging-in-Publication Data
Johnson, Russell, 1948–
Trouble at Christmas/by Russell Johnson:
illustrated by Bernadette Watts.
Summary: When Santa's rebellious reindeer desert him on Christmas
Eve, he must call on the lion, elephant, dragon, and other animals
to pull his sleigh for his important trip.
ISBN 1-55858-116-2
1. Santa Claus—Juvenile fiction.  [1. Santa Claus—Fiction.
2. Christmas—Fiction.  3. Animals—Fiction.]  I. Watts,
Bernadette, ill.  II. Title.
PZ7.J6365Tr  1991
[E]—dc20  90-28988

British Library Cataloguing in Publication Data
Johnson, Russell
Trouble at Christmas.
I. Title  II. Watts, Bernadette *1942–*
823.914 [J]

ISBN 1-55858-116-2

1 3 5 7 9 10 8 6 4 2
Printed in Belgium

# Trouble at Christmas

By Russell Johnson

Illustrated by Bernadette Watts

North-South Books / New York

"It's Christmas Eve again," grumbled Rhinehardt, the reindeer, to his wife Griselda. "Everyone in the world has fun on Christmas Eve, but all we do is work, work, work."

Griselda kicked angrily at the snow. "Why should we pull Santa Claus's sleigh every year?" she said. "We deserve a holiday, my love. Let's go home and visit our relatives."

The reindeer packed their bags, quietly shut the stable door behind them, and went away.

Nearby, Santa Claus had just finished loading all the presents into his sleigh.

"Griselda! Rhinehardt!" he called across to the stable. "Are you ready?"

There was only silence. Santa Claus then saw the footprints through the snow and his heart sank. "What will I do?" said Santa Claus. "Who will pull the sleigh?"

Horatio the mouse looked up at Santa Claus. "I will!" he said, flexing his muscles.

Santa Claus shook his head sadly. "You are far too small, my friend, but you've given me an idea. Let's ask the other animals to help! We can get the donkey, the camel, maybe even the elephant!"

All evening Santa Claus and Horatio visited various animals. The rabbit and the donkey were grumpy about being disturbed, but when Santa Claus explained the problem they agreed to help. A lion, a camel, and an elephant were all willing volunteers. Even the last dragon in the whole world was proud to join in.

It was getting dark and cold when everyone was assembled. Santa Claus was very happy, but when all the animals were together the problems began.

"Well," said the rabbit. "I'm the fastest, so I will take the lead."

"Never!" roared the lion. "I'm the king of beasts, so I will be first in line."

"Nonsense!" snorted the camel. "*I'm* used to long journeys, so I should lead."

"Excuse me," said the elephant quietly. "I'd like to point out that I'm the strongest. If you want *my* help you should let me be first."

"Stop this!" said Santa Claus sternly. "Christmas is no time for quarrelling. The dragon is going to lead us, since he can make fire and show us the way. Horatio will sit with me and read the map."

The old dragon was very proud to be asked to lead the sleigh. "I'm ready," he said as flames flashed out, singeing Santa Claus's beard. "Let's go."

Their travels went well at first, even though the mouse
suffered from a poor sense of direction. The dragon's flaming
breath shone in fantastically colored beams across the starry
sky and people in the North looked up and said, "Look, there
are the northern lights!"

Santa Claus and his helpers had many adventures, and some mishaps, on their travels round the world.

In northern Europe they delivered presents to a house with a thatched roof. While Santa Claus was quietly climbing down the chimney, the donkey began to munch the roof.

"Stop that!" commanded the dragon, but the greedy donkey took no notice and flipped his tail rudely in the dragon's face. The angry dragon flashed a great flame and the roof caught fire.

Luckily, the elephant raised his trunk and squirted out a fountain of water, putting out the fire in seconds.

"Well done," laughed Santa Claus, who had just reappeared. "Now, let's get on our way, and no more silly behavior!"

In one old townhouse Santa Claus found a welcome drink and a slice of cake someone's grandmother had put out for him. As he sat in a comfortable chair and ate the snack, the animals stamped around in the cold and grumbled about the delay.

In another country, the elephant slipped on a wet roof and dislodged several tiles. Luckily the camel cleverly caught the cascading tiles in his big underlip and together they mended the roof.

In a land of jungles and swamps the lion was nearly caught in a trap and sent to a zoo. Santa Claus told the lion to concentrate on the road and look where he was going.

On one of their last stops back in the North, they nearly got lost because Horatio was very tired and had great difficulty reading the complicated map.

The sky was just beginning to brighten on Christmas Day as the exhausted team finally arrived back at Santa Claus's home.

"Come on," said Santa Claus, rubbing his eyes. "Let's make something to eat."

All the animals grumbled. They were too tired to prepare a meal.

Inside the house chaos reigned. Santa Claus's kitchen was covered with flour, eggs, potato peels and apple sauce. Lumps of pastry drooped from the ceiling beams. The floor was awash with water and tomato sauce.

The two reindeer, who had been made to feel ashamed of deserting their work when they visited their relatives, had returned as fast as possible and were cooking a big Christmas meal to welcome the workers home and make up for their selfishness. Rhinehardt vigorously stirred a pot of stew while Griselda set the table and lit the Christmas candles.

Suddenly, just as a big casserole boiled over on the stove, in walked Santa Claus and his weary helpers.

Santa Claus stopped and stared in amazement. Then he laughed and laughed till his sides ached. All the animals laughed too.

Santa Claus was very happy his reindeer had returned, because even though they had behaved badly, he still loved them very much. He hugged Griselda and Rhinehardt and thanked them for preparing a Christmas meal.

"Well," said Santa Claus as everyone sat down to eat, "we had a little trouble this Christmas, but thanks to all of you things turned out pretty well."

With that, the animals smiled proudly, shook hands and enjoyed the best Christmas feast anyone had ever tasted.